BODEGA BOTANICA TALES: JOSE

BBT SERIES
BOOK 1

MARIA RODRIGUEZ BROSS

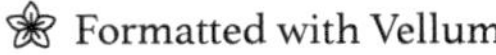 Formatted with Vellum

For the kids at the corner; I never forgot about you.

CONTENTS

1

———————

I met *them* back-in-the-day in Silk City. I was only eleven. Anytime I tell anybody about it, they think I'm traumatized by my past. I tell people it's not like that even though I wake up many a night, alone, in a pool of sweat trying to make sense of it all. I know what I saw. I just don't know if it was real. You tell me. I'll start from the beginning.

I heard about *her* from Carmen and Lucy, who would walk with me to and from school. Those girls pitied me back then. Lucy had warned me to be careful with the ghost lady in the back of the bodega sweeping her broom back and forth near the refrigerator aisle. Carmen said that Manny and his boys were spooked by her, and those boys didn't get scared by much. Everybody called her Chankla. That's Spanish slang for flip-flops, because she wore them even in the snow.

As we approached the bodega to buy candy, I held my books in one hand and checked if I had any spare change left over from that morning. I had none. I stopped and looked at Carmen and Lucy, discouraged.

Carmen shrugged her shoulders and said, "C'mon, I got you."

I smiled and Lucy opened the door for us.

If you are not well acquainted with a bodega, you might be surprised by the organized clutter of retro candies, dusty cleaning products, and nearly expired groceries colorfully packaged at inflated prices. When I was growing up, you could find one at every corner of the neighborhood; some might call it an eyesore between the unkept multi-family apartment buildings. Bodegas were a staple for people to purchase their buttered rolls with *café con leches*, a place open at the crack of dawn before the grown-ups headed out to their dead-end jobs. And then a few hours later, the lines at the counter would be replaced by kids waiting to purchase no-frill chips accompanied by artificially flavored juices, which caused tummy aches just in time for the grammar school bell. The allure of the array of products enticed me. I avoided staying in the bodega too long for fear of being shoved by the badly-behaved kids, like Manny, Tito, and Flaco, who were busy arguing with Bodega Man that day.

"You gave me a quarter and a nickel. I need another dime, knucklehead!" said Bodega Man.

"You're crazy! I gave you two quarters; give me back my change!" said Manny, who wore his jeans far below his waistline for any adult's liking. "I swear, man, if you don't give me back my change, I'm gonna get Chankla on your ass!"

Bodega Man grimaced and leaned in towards the counter, "Chankla?! You quit making up stories 'bout my bodega, you hoodlum!" said Bodega Man.

"They ain't stories! There's some lady that hangs around by the freezer box over there!" said Manny as he cocked his head to where I stood. Manny sneered at me and elbowed his friend, nodding in my direction. I tried to look away, but it was too late. They noticed my fixed stares of all of them. No one dared to talk to Bodega Man like Manny did.

Bodega Man was plump and bald. The bags under his eyes gave him a reason to quit pressing Manny for the money we all knew he probably owed.

Bodega Man threw the bag on the counter and said, "Know what? Take your pork rinds and get out! And don't be hanging out in front of my store!"

Manny and his boys took their goods and backed away from the counter.

"No hard feelings, but we don't stand in front of your store. We stand at the corner. It's a free country, right?" Manny said with a smirk.

Tito interrupted, "Hey, can I get one of those lucky bracelets that Chankla leaves on the counter?"

"Get outta here!" yelled Bodega Man as he shooed them away and waved us to him.

Lucy went up to the counter right away so Bodega Man wouldn't yell at her too. I stayed by Carmen, frozen, as Manny walked towards us.

"What you looking at?" he snapped and then immediately said, "What's up?"

"Nothin'," we said in unison, unsure which one of us was supposed to answer.

To my relief, Manny ignored me but he was so close I could smell the reefer on his breath. He leaned in too close to Carmen, which made me uncomfortable for her.

"Chankla's feet never turn blue in those sandals; it's mad crazy!" Tito said.

Manny rolled his eyes. "Man, why you always talking about ghosts? You know I'm powerful enough to scare her." I watched as Tito passed Manny a bottle of beer they had stolen. To this day, I couldn't believe they were only a year older than me. Then he waved goodbye to Carmen.

"Ain't you hear what I said?" Bodega Man glared at Manny and his friends. "Get out!"

Then he turned back to Lucy.

"Tell your moms that I can't keep selling you packs of cigarettes, you hear?" he said as he grabbed it from his locked cabinet and dropped it on the counter. He continued, "I don't like it when the cops question me about this."

"Yeah, I told her last time, but she said that you would be good with it," Lucy said.

"I'm not good with it! Your moms likes to lie a lot. That will be $2.25."

Lucy put two dollars on the counter and reached into her pocket but could not find the extra change she needed.

"You gotta be kidding me," said Bodega Man, "I ain't doing this today with you kids! You either got it or you don't."

Lucy looked back at us with concern. I could hear her heavy breathing.

"How much you need?" Carmen asked.

"A quarter," stuttered Lucy.

"Give her my quarter," I said.

I didn't want Lucy to get smacked by her mom for not bringing the cigarettes. I knew her mom would blame Lucy for losing the quarter even though we all knew she didn't give her enough money. Carmen asked if I was sure, and I was. Lucy needed the extra change more than me.

"C'mere kid," Bodega Man said.

"Me?" I said.

"Yeah, you."

And he motioned me to the counter.

I stepped up and he asked, "What's your name?"

"Jose Arce."

"Arce?"

Bodega Man somehow managed to have a slight smile while he gazed at me.

"You're Blanco's kid, right?"

"That's what they used to call him," I said all the while swaying on my feet and glancing back at Carmen and Lucy.

"You look just like him."

Bodega Man paused and tapped his finger on his closed lips. Then he said, "Listen, sorry about your sister. That's tough."

"She's alright," I said.

"I tell you what…"

He tapped his knuckles on the counter and then said, "You're a stand-up kid for giving your quarter away."

"It was never my quarter. Carmen was gonna hook me up," I said.

Lucy and Carmen stood there stunned by Bodega Man continuing to kindly talk to me. This was the same person who was rumored to have single-handedly grabbed a robber by his neck just to throw him on the sidewalk with the trash. He often called the police on anyone he disliked and enjoyed facing them in court just to say, "Good riddance, sucker". He didn't seem to care what anyone thought of him, since he protected what was his and would rather die than give up the treasure in his cash register.

That's why it surprised me when he said, "It's more reason why that's a stand-up thing to do."

He searched for something under the counter.

"Look, I know how much you kids like the *Now and Laters* and *Lemonheads* but it's not for free, but how about if I give you one of these bracelets?"

The collection of bracelets on the counter shone. The beads were sparkly and bright and covered all the colors of the rainbow.

"They're okay, I guess," I said feeling disappointed about the alternative.

The candy would've given me instant gratification.

What was I going to do with a bracelet meant for a girl? I thought.

He stared at me as if he were reading my mind.

"Maybe for your sister? They bring good luck."

His compassion made me uncomfortable.

"I don't know," I said.

Carmen jumped up and yelled to me, "Take the green-and-yellow one! It's pretty, Jose. Take it!"

Bodega Man leaned in towards me and acted like he knew me even though this was the first time he had ever spoken to me.

"Listen to your friend, Jose. Don't be like these knuckleheads out there, alright?"

I nodded. Never before had Bodega Man, or anyone for that matter, spoken to me like that. I grabbed the bracelet as fast as I could before Bodega Man could change his mind.

I looked back to say, "Thank you!"

Carmen and Lucy followed me out the door.

2

———

I hadn't seen my mother smile since Amelia was born. She was two, and still wasn't sitting, walking, or talking.

Mami and Papi would argue about it late at night when they thought I couldn't hear them. Mami would cry and say I wasn't like Amelia when I was her age and Papi didn't know what else he could do because he had to work so much. Mami wore pajamas all day long and did not bother to clean up after Amelia and me. Papi complained about it so I tried to help, but it was never in the right way.

The day after Bodega Man gave me the bracelet, I knocked on my parents' bedroom door. "Mami, are you there?" I said. "Mami?!"

Papi cracked the door open just enough for me to see that Mami was laying down again even though it was way past breakfast. Amelia was fussing in her crib.

"What now, Jose? I told you to grab the cornflakes!" Papi whispered and glanced at Mami.

"There's no milk," I said.

"… so you haven't eaten anything?" Papi said.

I shook my head. Amelia wailed and Papi grabbed her before she woke Mami up. But it was too late. Amelia was incessant with her cries.

"What's wrong with her?!" Mami said with a start. "I just put her down!" She tried to get out of bed but Papi stopped her.

"It's alright. I got it," Papi said. He cradled Amelia's floppy body to calm her down. Amelia had gotten too big, even for Papi's arms. She did not look like Mami and me; my sister had thick, straight black hair and fair skin like Papi.

"I have something for Mami," I said.

"Not now, Jose. Your Mami is resting!" Papi shouted in a whisper.

"… but I have something for her."

Papi handed me a five-dollar bill. "Just go down to the bodega and get the milk."

I was in disbelief. Papi never entrusted me with so much money before. "Really?!" I said.

"Yeah, Jose, don't make me regret this, and make sure to get the right change. Bodega Man overcharges for everything," he said while he paced back and forth with Amelia.

"Can I get pop rocks or bubble gum too?" I said.

"You see, that's gotta stop!" Papi closed the door behind him. "You don't need candy.

We need milk!"

"... but I did a good thing yesterday. I gave Lucy the money that Carmen was supposed to give me for candy," I said as I jumped up and down.

"What? Why you always hanging out with those girls?" Papi plopped Amelia down on the couch with pillows all around her. He tried to use the pillows to support her sitting, but she fell to her side every time.

"They're my friends, Papi. Why don't you like 'em?"

"I didn't say I don't like them... and why is Carmen giving you money, anyways? You can't be depending on girls for change. It don't look good." Papi closed his eyes, clenched his fists and sighed.

I froze and kept quiet, as my throat tightened and my face grew hot.

"Are you about to cry?" Papi shook his head.

"No!" I said, even though I felt the tears behind my eyes.

Papi sighed and lowered his voice. "C'mere."

I walked closer to him, but did not look him in the eye. Instead, I looked at Amelia, who never made eye contact with anyone. Papi knelt to my level, put his hands on my shoulders, and stared at me.

"I'm trying to teach you how to be a man. You're almost twelve years old and you gotta learn how to take care of business first. I'm counting on you... understand?"

I nodded while tears escaped me. I brushed them off hoping Papi wouldn't scold me.

The apartment walls were thin, so Papi stopped talking for a minute, since we heard, "What's the matter with Jose? I'll come out!"

Mami reappeared by the edge of her bedroom door.

"You see what I mean, Jose!" Papi walked over to Mami. "Watch your sister. I'll be right back."

While Papi talked to Mami in the other room, I whispered, "You need good luck Amelia; that's what Bodega Man said."

I wanted to make sure Mami and Papi would not hear me. I took out the bracelet from my pocket and showed it to Amelia, dangling it in front of her.

"Do you like it?"

To my surprise, she smiled and tried to grab it. I was stunned. Never before had Amelia tried to grab anything. I laughed out loud the second time she did it.

"Papi, Mami! Amelia just did something!"

But Amelia's smile turned into whiny cries.

"Shh!" Papi said as he rushed out and grabbed Amelia from the couch. "What did you do to her?"

Papi seemed angry so I put the bracelet back in my pocket. I jumped back to give him space.

"Nothin'! She just started crying."

I hated when Papi blamed me for Amelia's problems. I kicked some of her unused toys to the side and sat on the couch with a sullen look.

"Stop that nonsense! You gonna disturb your Mami again!"

It felt as if my presence was a bother.

"Where's the money I gave you?"

"It's in my pocket," I said.

"Then you need to get going!"

"To the bodega?"

Amelia arched her back, while Papi held her and she let out another cry. It was hard for us to hear each other, so he yelled, "Yeah! Go on! Help your Papi out, alright."

I looked up at him. Papi was sweating and had a strained look on his face. I realized that Papi used to be able to stand up to anybody, but Amelia had changed all that. He patted my back and walked away since he had better things to do. I opened the door of our tiny apartment while Mami came to retrieve Amelia from Papi's arms. She did not even notice that I was in the room.

Once I closed the door to my apartment building and walked onto the cold city sidewalk, my stomach started to hurt. Despite it all, I was determined to prove to Papi that I could be a man. I would get the milk and the change and make him proud. I was excited until I turned the corner.

Manny and his friends might be by the bodega, I thought.

I tried to ignore my cold hands, my growling hunger and my fear of seeing those boys.

3

When I got a block away from the bodega, I saw Manny and his boys standing on the corner with their fancy high-top sneakers. I bet they stole them. I saw small clouds of vapor appear near their mouths. I saw them put their hands in their pockets; I suspect trying to find warmth. Their chatter and laughter seemed cruel, even from a distance.

My plan was to bypass them on the curb and act as if I was not afraid. As I approached the corner, I tip-toed through the slushy snow as the sun was setting. That's when I heard Tito.

"Look at this kid wearing his high-waters!" He laughed and patted Manny on his back.

"Oh snap! High-waters for real!" said Manny. He was pointing and laughing at my pants.

I did not know what high-waters were, but all I knew was that I'd had these pants since Amelia was born. They used to be too long and now they left my ankles exposed. Mami forgot to pick up my new pants on layaway, so Papi decided to get the deposit back since money was tight. And then, I was left to defend myself, like a tough guy.

"They are not!" I kept walking. If I could just make it to the door, maybe Bodega Man would tell them to get out again.

"What you'd say to me?" Manny spat on the sidewalk.

"I said... they are not!" My teeth chattered as I sped up towards the bodega entrance.

Manny stomped up in front of me. "Hold him up against the wall!" hollered Manny.

Tito and another skinny boy they called Flaco grabbed me by the arms while my legs flailed. They pinned me against the wall of the bodega where the cheap siding was falling off and the brick was exposed.

"Please, don't do this!" I said, trying not to cry. Kids passing by saw what Manny was doing and kept walking. They were just happy it wasn't them.

"Check his pockets," ordered Manny.

"I got something good!" said Tito as he pulled out my five-dollar bill.

"You mean *we* got something good," Manny said, checking the corner to make sure Bodega Man did not come out with his bat.

"C'mon, Manny, you promised I could keep the next one!" Tito's grip loosened but I still could not escape his hold on me. I could see him dangling the five dollar bill from the corner of my eye.

Manny sighed. "Yo, switch with me. I'll check the other pocket."

When Manny came up behind me, I wailed like Amelia. Papi would be furious at my reaction, but I couldn't help it. Lucy had told me stories about how Manny would beat up boys and I couldn't believe I was about to be one of them.

Manny checked my pockets and that's when he said, "What the hell? You some kind of girl?" He had my green-and-yellow bracelet.

Tito and Flaco chuckled, while Manny squeezed my neck.

"No, it's for my sister. Give it back!" I could hardly breathe.

"I ain't giving you back nothing!"

Manny lifted the bracelet above his head as the streetlights turned on. The beads sparkled in the light, like diamonds.

"You think Carmen might like it? You're friends with her, right?" Manny said, continuing to pin me.

"Carmen wouldn't like it from you," I said under my breath.

"What'd you say to me?" Manny pressed my neck harder against the wall.

"Nothin'!"

Manny got behind me and yanked my pants down. "There! I fixed your high-waters," he said. "Wait, one more thing!" Manny grabbed my underwear and pulled up so hard that it gave me a wedgie.

"Aargh!" I yelled out in pain. "Help!"

"Help? Can't you see that I'm the one that helped you stop looking like a clown?"

Tito and Flaco laughed so loud that I was certain Bodega Man would hear them. But he didn't come out.

"I know you must like your butt cheeks showing for everybody to see!" Manny said.

"Tito, you still got that marker?"

"Thought you'd never ask," said Flaco.

"I wasn't talking to you!" said Manny. Flaco moved back.

Tito stopped laughing and the smile fell from his face. "Yeah, but don't you think that's enough?"

"We're not going to kick his ass. We'll write it so everyone else can do it," Manny said. "Tito, quick! Get me the marker! It's gonna be dark out soon."

Tito frowned and retrieved it from his back pocket. I could see Tito's pause but Manny snatched the marker out of his hand.

"No!" I yelled. "Please, I have to get milk for my family!"

Manny mocked me in a whiny voice by repeating what I just said. Flaco came over to hold me against the wall while Manny wrote on my butt cheeks. I sobbed. I had never felt so exposed or vulnerable. It was all too much.

"Yo," Tito said. "I think there's a *c* in 'kick'."

Tito scratched his head, and continued, "And is 'ass' spelled like that?"

Manny let go of me so he could clock Tito in the head. I was disappointed in myself for not taking the opportunity to run away. Instead, I stayed at that wall and lifted my pants while my whole body trembled.

"Man, this ain't school!" said Flaco.

Then I heard Tito say, "That hurt! Why'd you gotta do that?" Tito tripped back to protect himself from falling. "I'm just saying—"

"Shut up!" Manny cut Tito off.

Despite my fear, I wanted to stand up to Manny. I turned around and stood in front of him face to face.

"Give me back my money and my bracelet!" I said.

"Or what?" Manny said. He then shoved me against the wall and leaned in closer to me.

"... or else I'll get Chankla on you," I said under my breath.

"Whoa!" Tito and Flaco said in unison, each of them stepping back in surprise laughter.

"Who?"

Manny quickly put me in a headlock.

I struggled to get free, but it was no use. No one could hear me since it was so late. While tears ran down my face, I yelled out, "Chankla! Chankla!"

"You believed all that stuff Tito was talking about? You sure are a clown!" Manny continued, "Did I tell you to put your pants back on? I ain't done writing on your sorry ass!"

Manny forcibly turned my body around. I looked up and could see the crescent moon. It looked like it was watching me, as it shone on my humiliation. And that's when I heard heavy footsteps that slithered between raspy breaths, a being not of this world. I was just grateful that the sound was loud enough for Manny to let go of me.

"What's that?" Flaco said.

A silhouette of a woman came out of the bodega. The four of us gawked at her in a united front of terror. She moved at a slow pace like my grandmother. But once the moonlight shone on her, it was apparent that she was not old at all. Her skin was smooth with no evidence of hardship, like she had avoided the plight of being human. Her hair was coarse, like strings of curly thread.

Her eyes were sunken with pupils that glistened like roasted coffee beans. She wore a long, emerald-green dress that covered her knees; a *bata*. Her feet were adorned by green sandals with a tiny white orchid near the crevice of the big toe. She slowly walked towards us.

"Yo, that's Chankla!" I heard Tito say in front of me. He coughed and coughed.

"I can't breathe," said Flaco. "Let's get outta here!"

And the next thing I saw was Tito and Flaco run down the street. They didn't look back, not even for Manny. I couldn't believe Manny was left behind with me. I was sure we would die together once Chankla got a hold of us.

Manny soon backed away from me, but could not make himself run. He foamed at the mouth, then dropped to the sidewalk, and gasped for air. The bracelet he stole from me fell from his hand and landed right between my legs. His eyes wept a seedy, black curd. I also fell to the ground sure this would be the beginning of the end.

"You called." Her voice was deep and candid. She commanded the space of the corner as if it was hers. The moonlight served as a spotlight on her tight, curly hair that neatly parted in the middle.

"I did?"

I was relieved that I could speak, since I thought I lost my voice. I shook my head a few times to make sure I was not dreaming. She took my hand and helped me get up.

"Do you want your bracelet back?" she said.

We watched Manny struggle to get up from the ground.

"I do," I said, "but I need my five dollars more."

"I'm afraid that's gone," Chankla said bluntly.

She picked up the bracelet with the tips of her fingernails and handed it to me.

"I recommend you put it on your wrist, instead of trying to give it to others," she said.

I put it on right away. I wanted to leave but Manny kept falling back down and crying out for help. I tried to help Manny stand, but he was too heavy for me to lift on my own. I looked at Chankla for help.

"Leave him!" Chankla said. "All downfalls need time to rise!"

I did not know what she meant, but I was too scared to question her orders. I was afraid for my own life, even though I was mesmerized by the colorful beaded bracelets she wore along both her arms. I thought this might be my best chance to leave so I turned my back to her.

"Haven't you forgotten something?" she said.

I stopped and closed my eyes.

"Come with me. I will help you get milk," she said.

And with that, Chankla turned away from me and walked towards the bodega entrance.

After all, Papi would be upset if I returned with nothing. I could not catch up to Flaco and Tito, who would never return my money.

I had to follow Chankla.

4

When I entered the bodega, it was no longer the place I remembered. The shelves were full, but instead of goods and items they were filled with species of plants I had never seen before. My eyes could not distinguish between all of the vibrant shades of green; everything camouflaged into one big beautiful existence.

As Chankla guided me through the brightly lit aisle, I noticed that the endless rows of refrigerators were no longer ordinary appliances. The edges and handles were made of gold and the light coming from them felt warm, like sunlight.

In front of each door was a stand-alone telescope, permanently mounted on tree trunks.

"Take a look," Chankla said.

I leaped forward with excitement. She seemed pleased with my curiosity. When I peeked through, I saw men and women, who looked like farmers milking cows and collecting eggs. They carried the jugs of milk and baskets of eggs to the shelves within. I jumped back; I had to be hallucinating.

"You'll get the milk later. Follow me," said Chankla.

Even though I was fascinated by the beauty all around me, I still wanted to leave. I felt guilty about staying there knowing that Mami and Papi would have something else to worry about besides Amelia.

Did they take Bodega Man away? Will they do the same to me? I thought.

"You are safe," said a voice close to where Chankla and I were walking. "Bodega Man is not here," continued the being I could not see.

"How did you know that I was thinking about him?" I said, wondering if Chankla could hear the voice too.

"We share all things here, even our thoughts," the being said.

"Where are you?" I asked in my loudest voice, feeling excitement instead of fear.

"You can always find me near the flamboyán trees."

Chankla and I continued down an aisle that morphed into rows of tall plants, which nearly touched the ceiling. When we turned the corner, the walls transformed into woven cane and there were beautiful gardens and orchards waiting for us. The flowers were bright and colorful while the trees were filled with wild fruits I'd never seen before. At the end of that aisle was a domed flamboyán tree covered in rich, red flowers, that extended horizontally. The tree's breathtaking panoramic view held me spellbound for a moment only to be interrupted by the sight of a bony man sitting at the end of the tree's bloom. He was sitting on a three-legged stool and clutching a cane. He had long, white hair separated into twelve thick strands, each wrapped in dried-up plantain leaves. A mongoose lounged easily on his shoulder. When I got closer, the mongoose perked up and acted more like the guard dogs in my neighborhood. The man's eyes were different, not human. The color of the iris was blue, like the water along the Caribbean shores, but the pupils were shaped like seashells. He wore dozens of cowries and colorful beaded necklaces.

"You have come for milk?" he said.

"Yes," I eagerly responded.

The patterns and endless shades of green around me filled my vision. I could not focus my attention on any one thing since it was all so lush and spectacular.

"I think I'm lost; I was looking for the bodega."

"This is a bodega," he said.

"... but you told me Bodega Man wasn't here," I said.

"He's not. I'm afraid we're his competition, and no bodega man likes that."

He stood up and clutched a cane for support. His height intimidated me but I faced him anyway. The mongoose scampered down his back and scurried towards me. It was a bit larger than a cat, the kind that would wander around Silk City at night.

"And who are you?"

"I'm Wicho. It's an honor to meet you," he said.

He opened his arms wide and bowed deeply.

I got a closer look at him and couldn't believe the vision before me. He was gowned in what looked like a brown, luminous robe long enough to meet his feet. The sleeves were flared, but connected back to his frame when he wasn't moving. The most amazing part was the different compartments of tiny palm leaves adorning the front of his chest, each with its own button, shaped like bees.

His patience and kindness were evident. "Wicho?" I said.

"That's *Don* Wicho," said Chankla. She bowed her head towards him with a smile. "We respect our elders in this bodega and that little creature you see is Luna."

"Yes, I know... I mean, yes," I said. I hadn't meant to be rude. Chankla left my side and wandered off to smell the orchids behind me.

"Which bodega am I in? It looks different from the one I was in yesterday," I said.

"Did Chankla not explain?!"

I shook my head.

"Oh, I do apologize. We need to give you a proper greeting," Don Wicho said. He hung his cane on a tree branch in front of him and commanded Luna to join Chankla. Luna did not look pleased, but she obeyed anyway.

Don Wicho walked a bit ahead of me, turned around, and bowed. "Welcome to the *Bodega Botanica!*"

"Botanica? What's that?" I said.

Don Wicho grabbed his cane again to keep from losing his balance.

"It's a place where you can find plants, of course. Look at the guava trees and tamarind bushes."

My eyes widened as I took in the view surrounding me. There was no end to this magical wonderland.

How would I explain this to Papi or anyone for that matter? I thought.

"Explanations aren't always needed," said Don Wicho. I'd forgotten that he could read my thoughts.

I continued to try and make visual sense of the rows of colorful flowers, life-size potted plants and trees towering above me. I stopped to admire a striking leaf and took a closer look at its delicate nature. Don Wicho put his hand on his hip, and leaned into his cane and watched me.

"Those are tobacco plants, but not the kind Lucy purchased for her mother," he said.

"How do you know about that?"

"You were wondering about it, weren't you?"

Don Wicho looked at me for confirmation and I agreed. I quickly learned to control my thoughts since they were there for them to see. Oddly, I wanted my privacy back so I immediately spoke without thought.

"... but I can find milk here, like in a bodega?"

"This bodega is unique. You see, we believe that a bodega is nothing without a *botánica*. How can you have one without the other? A *botánica* is the great life force. It holds all the power in the world."

Don Wicho's words made me feel powerless. I blamed it on not having eaten all day.

"I'm sorry, but I have to excuse myself. I'm hungry and need to get home."

"Hungry?" said Don Wicho.

I was motionless and silent. I lacked the energy to respond. I shook my head in an effort to stay focused, but suddenly collapsed into a deep sleep anyway.

When I woke up, Luna tried to get my attention by licking my bare ankles between the bottom of my high-waters and the top of my sneakers. I was too exhausted to be afraid. I sat up and rubbed my eyes and soon realized that the *Bodega Botanica* apparently was not a dream after all. It was still all around me.

"You poor boy!" said Don Wicho as he towered above me. Chankla was there too and she bent down to feel my head. When she was satisfied, she assisted me in standing. She looked around and pulled fruit from one of the trees.

"Here, eat!"

"I don't know how to eat that," I said, shaking my head.

"It's *quenepa*. You can easily peel with your fingers," said Don Wicho. He requested some from Chankla and demonstrated how to break the outer green shell and showed me the furry, slimy, yellow stuff inside. I was too overwhelmed to take it from them.

I craved familiarity, but was unable find it in this place, full of abundance. There were too many things I did not know and taking fruit from a stranger would just make my Papi angry.

Chankla sighed and put the *quenepas* back on the tree.

"We don't waste anything here," she said and soon disappeared back into the rows of *quenepa* trees.

Don Wicho seemed annoyed and called out, "Chankla, come back!" When she did not respond, he shouted again, "Chankla!"

"You call her that too?" I regretted asking, as I wasn't sure if I was being disrespectful.

"Of course! Who do you think whispered her name to the boys on the corner?" Don Wicho chuckled.

"You called?" said Chankla.

She suddenly appeared and I hadn't expected her to be so close to me. I screamed and jumped back, stepping on Luna, who made a mournful screeching sound.

"I'm so sorry!" I said.

Luna scurried back to the safety of Don Wicho's shoulder.

"She's always in the way. You spoil that mongoose," said Chankla.

"You answered my call!" said Don Wicho.

"Don't I always? What can I get for you?" she said.

"The boy still needs to eat! ... maybe something his mother

makes him?" Don Wicho said, pensive. "I've got it!" He clapped his hands. "Can you make *mofongo*?"

"Of course," said Chankla, "follow me."

She guided us with the wave of her hands. As I walked side-by-side with Don Wicho, he leaned in and whispered to me, "I used to be just like you, though it may be hard to believe." He paused ever so often to prune a few plants while he spoke of all the medicinal uses the plants had to offer.

"Excuse me, Don Wicho..."

"Go on."

"Can a *botánica* help me?" I said.

"Of course! What is it that you want?" Don Wicho said.

While I pondered my response, I looked ahead. I could see that Chankla was placing our meals at the bodega counter, except that this one was lit with candles instead of fluorescent lights.

"I want my five dollars back," I said.

We were not far away when Chankla interjected. "I'm afraid that's not possible. It is in direct contrast with two of our four *Bodega Botanica* rules."

"What rules?" I said, looking around in disappointment. My stomach hurt.

Don Wicho said, "Look there in front of you, above Chankla's head."

The rules were written on a chalkboard, the kind that stretched all along a single wall like in a classroom. A swarm of fireflies lit up the writing:

The Bodega Botanica Rules

Rule 1: *No exchange of money.*

Rule 2: *Take only what you need.*

Rule 3: *Wish for the future.*

Rule 4: *Accept your karma.*

Not only was I famished, but now I had to be concerned with rules. My wonder had turned to worry.

Why I am here? Who are these beings? ...and why are they interested in me instead of Manny and his boys? They are the ones that need to learn how to follow rules!

I looked back at Don Wicho and asked, "Why do you have them written up there like that?"

"For you to remember," said Don Wicho as he moved around smelling all the species of tropical flowers on the counter. "Like Chankla said, you cannot wish for something that is in the past, that's rule number three."

Don Wicho finally sat down on a barstool facing Chankla, who was busy mixing something in a mortar three times larger than my head.

Then he said, "Come, sit."

Don Wicho patted the straw-topped wooden stool next to him.

I sat and Chankla served the *mofongo* in a small wooden bowl. My stomach rumbled at the sight of it.

"Eat!" Chankla commanded.

Don Wicho scooped a small amount for Luna, but she refused it and scurried away to lay on a nearby tiny hammock. I, on the contrary, devoured it with my hands, relishing the sweetness of the mashed plantains mixed with the salty, crispy pork skin. It was divine. Once I finished eating, Don Wicho gazed at me as if I were someone important. I was so confused by his adoration. I mean, couldn't even stand up to Manny.

"I must ask again, what is it that you want?" he said leaning intently on the counter.

Chankla stopped pulverizing the plants with her pestle and waited for my response.

"Can you help my Mami?" I said.

"I'm afraid I cannot help her either." He continued to smile. "That's part of rule number two. You and only _you_ can take what you need. Your mother would have to come here herself should she need our help. Understand?"

"No! I don't understand!" I shoved the bowl away and glared at the counter. "You can't get my five dollars! You can't help my Mami! My skin grew hot with anger. I scowled at the wild palm leaves that covered the ceiling and the coconuts that hung from every corner. "What are you good for if you can't actually help me?"

Chankla dropped the mortar and pestle. The deep thud of it slamming onto the counter vibrated in my chest. I was too scared to keep complaining.

"Respect your elders," she said, glaring at me.

After a long pause, she poured the contents of the mortar into small green sachets. Next, she gathered the sachets and organized them into a larger arc behind her, resembling a rainbow. In my silence, I marveled at their radiance. The beauty of it made me feel ugly. I didn't belong here.

"I'm sorry. It's just that..." I placed my hands on my face. I could no longer contain my frustration. Don Wicho covered his thin lips with the spread of his fingers and waited.

"There, there," he said, "crying releases useless energy."

I reached into my pocket and pulled out the bracelet.

"I wanted to give her this bracelet. I don't have change for Papi. I'm supposed to be home, with the milk. I'm in so much trouble!"

I threw the bracelet on the counter and buried my head in between my hands.

"Now, now, it will be fine," said Don Wicho as he continued to pat my back. "I never said that I could not help you. I only told you to read the rules. Now, think it through. What is it that you really want?"

"You mean rule number three?" I swallowed my tears, but I could not stop crying. Don Wicho unbuttoned one of his leaves on the right side of his body and handed me a handkerchief that he pulled directly from one of the chambers of his beating heart. I gasped in astonishment and turned away. I did not want Don Wicho to think that I did not appreciate his gesture.

I continued, "Can you make Manny stop hurting me? Can you make him go away?"

"Are you sure that's what you want to do?" said Chankla.

"Don't question the boy!" said Don Wicho. "This is the first time I see a glimmer of confidence."

"Read rule number four, again," said Chankla. "Are you prepared to live with the consequences of your wish; that's the meaning of karma."

I looked at Chankla and then at Don Wich and said, "I don't need to read it. I'm sure that's what I want!" It served him right for what he did to me."

I wiped my tears away with my arms and waited anxiously for Don Wicho's response.

"I see," said Don Wicho. "You have abided by all the rules and therefore we can stop Manny from ever hurting you again. This, I promise you."

Chankla turned to face Don Wicho.

"Let the boy join me," she said.

Don Wicho agreed with a nod. Luna was awakened out of her slumber by the sudden silence. She pranced out of her hammock and watched us with anticipation.

Chankla reached behind the counter to retrieve a sachet and walked around to meet me on the other side. She slowly poured the contents of the sachet on the ground until she made a perfect circle. She then stood in the middle and asked me to get off the stool and step into the circle.

"Don't forget to put on your bracelet," she said.

I obeyed without question. I would have done anything to make my wish come true. When I finally met her in the circle, she held my hands and led me to kneel in front of her so we could face each other. She poured the rest of the contents into the palm of her hand.

"This is the *ya-fe*, for your wish," Chankla said, with a grin.

"What is *ya-fe*?" I said.

"It is a dust derived from some of the plants in this *botánica*," Chankla said.

"Which ones?" I said.

"The ones you need," said Don Wicho, as he stood outside the circle, watching us.

"What do you do with it?" I said.

Chankla moved towards me and said, "You blow the *ya-fe* to me and I will blow it back to you. This is the life force that you need to make your wish come true. It's that simple."

Don Wicho looked on with amusement, as if he were watching a baseball game, like my Papi.

My tears dissipated.

I blew the *ya-fe*, as they called it, to Chankla and she in turn blew the *ya-fe* back to me. I stopped only to watch the *ya-fe* all around us, as it rose and swirled in a motion that made me giddy. I could no longer see Don Wicho. I turned to Chankla and we continued to blow the *ya-fe* back and forth. Each time, I felt more and more joyful, and the bodega around us shifted and blurred as if I were in a dream. We were both laughing and I soon felt weightless, and then suddenly, I was standing alone in front of the refrigerators right where I had initially entered, the bodega. It was quiet.

I remembered rule number two.

Take only what you need.

I looked down and the bracelet was still on my wrist. Since Chankla was no longer with me, I took off the bracelet and put it in my pocket. I opened the sliding refrigerator door, grabbed the jug of milk, and ran all the way home.

5

When I got back to the apartment, the door opened and I nearly slammed right into Papi. He was furious. Papi scolded me for taking nearly five hours to get milk. Mami had been asking about me and Papi was just about to come looking for me. I didn't know what to say. It had only felt like I was gone for half an hour. When Papi asked where I was, I told him I didn't know, which only made him angrier.

"I'm sorry, Papi," I said.

"Things gotta change with you, Jose," he said. "Get in here!"

I did not know where to begin once I entered the apartment. It was the first time I noticed the stained, cracked ceilings and the pots full of water directly beneath them. My home was a far cry from the *Bodega Botanica*. Papi grabbed the jug of milk from my arms.

"Jose, I asked you a question! What took you so long?"

"I'm sorry, Papi! I guess I was distracted," I said. I wanted to tell the truth but I knew the truth would sound like a lie.

"And you got my change, right?" said Papi as he prepared a bowl of cornflakes for me on the table. I was terrified to tell him the truth of why I didn't have his money.

"I'm not hungry," I said. I trembled and that's when it happened: a warm wetness dripped down my legs and pooled at my feet. I couldn't move.

"Of course you ar—" Papi froze mid-sentence when he saw me. "Why would you pee all over the floor!"

"I don't have any change, Papi," I said. I stood there without moving any part of my body, trying not to cry again. I looked him in the eye this time.

"What else did you buy?" Papi said. He walked over and shook me by my arms, as if the change would drop out from my body. The bracelet fell instead.

"Stop!" Mami said. She stood at the bedroom door, watching us. We both stared at her as she spoke.

"Why are you yelling at him? He peed his pants, so what? I used to do that too at his age and then my father would beat me for it. Is that what you plan to do to him?"

"Of course not," said Papi. We were both stunned to see that Mami was dressed in clothes other than her nightgown and had brushed her hair back in a neat bun. Mami walked past Papi and faced me.

"It's alright. It's just an accident." I felt comforted by Mami; it was like I had her back again.

"I'm sorry, Mami." I did not want to make anything worse for her. She had enough troubles with Amelia.

"Don't be sorry. Amelia will pee in her pants for the rest of her life but no one will ever get mad at her, right?" she said.

"Right." I lowered my head.

"What's this?" Mami picked up the sparkling bracelet adorned with beads of green and yellow.

"Is this why you don't have any change?" Papi said.

"It's beautiful, Jose." Mami put her hand on my shoulder and crouched down so we could be eye to eye. "But Papi's right. Why did you buy this?"

"I didn't buy it! Bodega Man gave it to me. I swear!"

Papi paced back and forth. "It's more like he took your money."

"Could you stop?" said Mami, glaring at Papi. "Jose, why would Bodega Man give you such a thing?"

I didn't want to answer.

"Jose?" Mami said firmly.

"It's all because of Amelia," I said.

"What about Amelia?" Mami said. I remained silent. Mami held my shoulders. "Jose, what did he say about Amelia?!"

"Nothin'," I said. Mami took a deep breath. She turned away, let go of me, and patted my shoulders. Then she pointed her finger at Papi. "I told you they were talking about her. Everyone knows." As she closed her eyes, tears spilled down her cheeks. She walked over, sat down on the couch, and covered her face with her hands.

"Mami, don't cry, please!"

"Then why won't you tell me?" Mami said. Papi sat on the couch and put his arm around Mami's shoulder. Papi snapped his fingers and pointed to me.

"Go! Now! In the bathroom and change. Get them wet pants off!"

"But, Papi," I said and tried to approach them.

"You are not getting this bracelet back," Papi said and he pointed again towards the bathroom.

"But Amelia liked it. Let me show you," I said.

Mami wiped her tears. "You can't wake her up right now, Jose."

"You don't believe Amelia liked it, do you?" I said.

But Mami told me not to argue with her, that we were going to church tomorrow. That made Papi mad. They argued about what was wrong with our family and I waddled to the bathroom to clean myself up.

"Are you ignoring me?" said Mami, right before I closed the bathroom door.

Papi answered. "Nah! I'm checking on our kid, who just peed all over our floor."

Papi knocked on the bathroom door.

"Jose, open up!"

"I need to wash his pants," said Mami.

"I know." Papi continued knocking. "Jose, what's the matter? Let me in."

I opened the door. When Papi stepped into the bathroom, I could not look him in the eye.

"I can't get it off," I said.

"Get what off?"

"These boys on the corner, they—"

"They what?" Papi said.

"On my back, my butt even—"

"Turn around. Let me see!"

Papi saw what Manny and the boys did to me and got very quiet. Papi sat on the toilet seat and read aloud, *"kik my azz"*. He was silent for a long while as I scrubbed at the marker on my skin.

Mami knocked on the door. "Hand me the pants. It's getting late and I want to make sure we have them in time for church tomorrow."

Papi got up and handed mami the pants but then closed the door again.

"Don't let Mami know what they did to you," he whispered without looking at me.

"Papi?" I said, and he looked at me then to let me know I could continue. "Bodega Man said we need good luck, because of Amelia."

Papi closed his eyes and shook his head. He walked over to the bathtub and turned on the faucet. He sat at the edge of the bathtub and let the warm water flow on his fingers to ensure that it would not be too cold for me. He handed me a clean washcloth.

"There, it will be ready soon."

Papi stood up, lowered his head and walked towards the door, but before he opened it, he said, "I don't need a bracelet to know I have good luck. My good luck is your mother, Amelia, and you. Wash up, put your pajamas on, and get to bed. We'll deal with this in the morning."

He walked out and closed the door behind him.

6

———

The next morning, Papi and I walked to the bodega, but we could not find it. Papi asked someone on the street and they pointed us to a different location two blocks further away. Papi scratched his head.

When we entered the store, my heart was pounding. I searched for evidence of my experience in the *Bodega Botanica*, but found none. Everything was the same as the day I entered with Carmen and Lucy except that it was unusually empty. Bodega Man was reading his newspaper. After Papi cleared his throat to get his attention, Bodega Man put down the newspaper and asked what he could get us. Then he recognized Papi.

"Yo! Wassup, Blanco?... and it's Jose, right?" Bodega Man smiled at me. "It's been a long time since I seen you. How you been?"

"I'm alright," said Papi. "I've seen better days, but um, weren't you on East 16th Street?"

"Nah! We've always been on 18th," said Bodega Man.

"Yeah?" Papi looked around. "I could have sworn you were down the street."

"Nah!... always been here," Bodega Man said. "What can I do for you?"

Papi put my bracelet on the counter. "My son bought this here and we want to return it."

Bodega Man looked confused. "Alright, but I never sold him the bracelet."

"What?" Papi glared at me. "He stole it or something?"

"I didn't steal nothin'," I said.

"Nah, I gave it to him," said Bodega Man.

"Gave it to him? I suppose you gave him the milk too?" Papi said.

"The milk?" said Bodega Man.

"Yeah, he was here yesterday and bought milk, right?"

"No, definitely not yesterday." Bodega Man pursed his lips and shook his head. "You didn't hear what happened?"

Bodega Man explained that his bodega was closed yesterday. Then he continued, "Cops were all over the streets and the surrounding bodegas were closed too."

"How about those boys on the corner?" Papi asked.

"Ah! you mean Manny and those knuckleheads?" Papi nodded his head. "Cops picked them up too," Bodega Man said.

I couldn't believe it. I wanted to leave in case Chankla showed up to tell him that it was me who wished it upon those boys. I tugged at Papi's arm, but he ignored me and continued talking.

"For what? They're like Jose's age."

Bodega Man gestured with his hands. "I dunno."

"They locked them up?" Papi asked.

Bodega Man nodded.

"For loitering?" Papi looked surprised.

I stood up on my toes and looked to the back of the store to try to and get a glimpse of Chankla. She wasn't there.

"I guess so, but I'm glad to not see their sorry asses standing in front of the store no more, so if you ask me, they did me a favor." Papi became quiet. "You alright, Blanco?" Bodega Man asked.

"Yeah, it's just... didn't we used to do the same thing?"

Bodega Man shrugged. "I know, but these kids today be selling out there in broad daylight."

"They were selling? ... really?" Papi continued.

"Not sure, but these kids got no discretion."

"And we did?" Papi sighed with disbelief.

"I mean, yeah. I heard some of them are starting to carry guns," Bodega Man said.

Papi looked around as if he was trying to find answers in all the clutter that the bodega had to offer. We noticed the line forming behind us.

"Anything else I can help you with?" said Bodega Man.

"Yeah, I'll get a few pieces of bubble gum," Papi said.

As Papi and I left the bodega, he said, "Jose, this is the last time I'm going to ask you about this and don't lie to me. Where were you yesterday?"

"At the bodega, Papi!"

"Which one?"

"The one on 16th Street, I swear!"

Papi eyes darted anxiously at me before scanning the surrounding city blocks. He pushed his lustrous hair and clasped his hands around his neck as he turned away from me.

"Are you ok, Papi?"

"I'm ok," he said.

In hindsight, I now realize that he wasn't okay and just as frightened as I was on that day. We both knew that bodega was never on 18th Street.

"I don't want to hear nothin' about this day, you hear?"

I nodded in agreement, even though it made me feel sick. We continued on our walk and that's when Papi handed my bracelet back to me along with a piece of bubble gum.

"I believe this belongs to you," he said. Papi put the other piece of bubble gum in his mouth and started chewing and said, "I forgot how good this is."

I put the bracelet back on my wrist right way, since I remembered Chankla's advice to me. My thoughts were interrupted by Papi, who continued, "Mami and I were gonna tell you after church. We're moving at the end of the month, so that Abuela can help Mami with Amelia."

I stopped walking and said, "What about Carmen and Lucy?"

"What about them?" said Papi.

"They're my friends."

"You'll make new friends."

Papi's response sounded simple, but as the years went on, I soon found out that it would be more complicated to make those kinds of friends again. Despite getting my wish granted at the *Bodega Botanica*, I was still that kid with the high-waters, nervous, afraid and alone. As we started walking again, Papi told me that we were meeting Mami, Amelia and Abuela. We crossed the street to meet them in front of the church and that was the second time Amelia grabbed my hand to get to my bracelet.

"You see, Papi," I said, "Amelia is moving her hand!" Everyone was happy to see that and I felt like I had done a good thing.

When I entered the church, I sat next to Abuela, Papi, Mami, and Amelia. I said a prayer for the very first time, acting on rule number four: *accept your karma.*

I would wait for it like a man should.

7

———

But as the years passed, the guilt about my wish weighed on me. It was twenty years later that I was at a bar in Manhattan waiting for a guy who had contacted me online. He said he knew me from back in the day and needed to urgently talk to me. I didn't recognize his face or name, but he said he knew Carmen. I hoped maybe he could connect me with her in some way, so I had agreed to meet him.

While I waited, I pulled out the green-and-yellow bracelet from my wallet. I kept it there like some people keep a rabbit's foot or a porcelain elephant in their pocket. It was good luck. I closed my eyes and held it close to my heart, thinking about how I never saw Carmen and Lucy again after moving away from the neighborhood.

"What will it be?" said the bartender.

I ordered a rum and coke and thought about my life and my karma. I never got wedgies again, but I was ignored by my peers after we moved. I was anxious and felt out of place most days. How could I ever explain the *Bodega Botanica*? Most days I thought I dreamt it all.

"Are you Jose?" A man approached and offered me a handshake.

"Yeah, Jose Arce," I said.

He looked familiar but I could not put a name to the face. He had a full beard and looked like he weighed about three hundred pounds.

"Nestor Espinoza," he said.

He was breathing heavily but managed to sit in the barstool next to me. I asked if he wanted a drink and he ordered a club soda. I couldn't help but make a face at that.

Who orders a soda at a bar? I thought.

But he explained he was in recovery and then I felt terrible. If I had known, I would have picked a different place.

"Oh, no worries. It doesn't bother me; it's been years since I've had a taste for it," he said with a smile.

The bartender brought over our drinks and he said, "But that's why I'm here; I'm doing my AA steps... you know, Alcoholics Anonymous."

"What does that have to do with me?" I sipped my drink and looked at my watch.

"Well, you're from Silk City, right? You had a baby sister who was sick or something like that?"

"Yeah, Amelia. She's not sick; she has autism."

I didn't want to talk about my sister with him. He was practically a stranger.

He twisted the straw in his drink and lowered his head. "How's she doing?"

"She's good, happy all the time. She lives with my parents and goes to a day program," I said. "Listen, no disrespect, but I don't know you, so I don't want to talk about my sister."

"You don't recognize me?" he said.

"Frankly, no." I looked him in the eye.

"Well, I did put on a good amount of weight." He laughed and gestured to his stomach. "It's me... Flaco!"

"Fla-Flaco?" I took a quick gulp of my drink. I felt uncomfortable since all I wanted to do was punch this guy in the face.

"Yeah, everyone called me that back in the day 'cause I was so skinny."

"I remember now," I said.

"But like I said, I'm doing the steps and I wanted to meet you in person so I could apologize."

Man, this is crazy! I thought.

I hated this guy for having to bring up the past when all I wanted to do was forget it. I looked over my shoulder and scanned the room in case there were any further surprises. My right hand unconsciously clenched into a fist and my left leg started to fidget.

"Apologize? F-For what?"

"Well, you know... what we did to you," said Flaco, who hung his head and held his glass with both hands.

"Awe! That?" I searched for all the pretty girls in the room to distract myself from the pit in my stomach. "I've been over that. We were kids. I'm sorry you had to waste your time coming all the way down to a bar when you're trying to stay sober. I mean..." I laughed nervously. "Anyway, it wasn't really you, it was..."

I took a sip of my drink and put my hand over my head, then my face so I could pretend to have time to think.

"Manny," said Flaco.

"Yeah, that's it," I said.

"You heard what happened, right?" Flaco said.

"No."

I folded my arms and Flaco kept talking.

"We ain't have any drugs on us. We weren't selling anything, but we were drunk that day. That's for sure!"

Flaco took a sip of soda and wiped his mouth with his hand.

"You talking about the drug raid, but I'm talking about something else," I said.

"What do you mean?" said Flaco.

I couldn't believe this guy. He comes all the way down here to apologize to me but he doesn't remember seeing the ghost lady.

"You don't remember leaving Manny while Tito and you ran off?"

Flaco shook his head and looked at me like I was the crazy man.

"The lady?" I asked.

"What lady? I ran off? No! I just know what we did to you and I'm sorry about that but I don't remember us running off. Last thing I remember, we saw you run home holding a jug of milk."

"What?" I leaned back in my barstool in disbelief.

I wasn't about to let this guy make me feel like a fool. As he continued speaking, I stopped listening for a minute. I wondered if I had fabricated the entire story in my mind. Although, I disliked this conversation, I soon got back into it.

"So what happened to you that day?"

"Cops locked us up for nothing," said Flaco. "They questioned all of us about that corner and what we seen on the block. Tito and I didn't flinch. We kept to our story that we ain't seen nothin'...but Manny...he must have said something, because it got back to somebody who didn't like it."

"How so?" I said.

"Someone knew he snitched. Some gang members beat him down so bad that he ended up using a wheelchair— till this day," said Flaco.

"Oh yeah?" I said, rapidly losing interest.

I wondered why I continued to ask questions I didn't want answers to. I felt emotionally detached from everything Flaco was telling me. There was a part of me that felt guilty for Manny getting his own karma.

That's rule number four, I thought.

I flagged the bartender for the bill since I couldn't stand one more minute being there with someone who denied part of what had happened that day. I felt like I was losing my mind. There was no way this guy could remember what he did to me, but yet forget <u>her</u>.

"It was cool catching up with you, but I gotta get going," I said.

I stood up and took my wallet out.

"Let me get this," Flaco said. "We took your money that day."

"No, don't worry about it," I said. He gesture got on my nerves, but I stayed cool.

"It's part of my steps. Please, let me pay you back." Flaco put the five-dollar bill on the counter and looked me in the eye. It didn't change my mind about him.

"...but you really don't remember seeing her?"

"Who?" said Flaco.

"Nobody," I said, annoyed and disgusted. "If it helps you any, thanks for the apology."

I got up and walked towards the exit.

But I stopped in my tracks after he said, "Wait! You ever talk to Carmen?"

"Carmen." I said. He had my full attention. It had been twenty years since I last saw Carmen, but not a day goes by that I don't think about her. I wonder if she ever thinks about me. I imagine what I would say to her if I saw her again and then I am reminded of my time at the *Bodega Botanica.*

How could I tell her about Don Wicho and Chankla without her thinking that I'm delusional? I thought.

"What about her?" I said. Flaco didn't deserve to know how I really felt.

"She's still friends with Manny. Isn't that crazy?"

"Yup. That's crazy alright since from what I remember, they were never friends."

Flaco shook his head from side to side and then he said, "I thought I'd reach out to her, so I can make things right with Manny too, but..."

"But what?" I interrupted his thought process.

Flaco blocked me with his hand to stop me from moving further. I brushed his hand aside and got up.

"No disrespect, I have to go."

I started to walk away, but then he said, "There's something else I need to tell you."

He jumped up from his seat and caught up with me. He coughed and leaned against the wall where I stood.

I did not ask him if he was alright.

"What?" I said, trying to keep myself from feeling more annoyed than I already was. I adjusted my coat. He leaned in and I stepped back and sighed.

"Juvi was rough, being locked up, especially at the age we were..."

"I bet," I said.

"They put us in isolation to break us, you know. We cried for our mothers, but not Manny."

"He didn't have a mom, grandma?"

"No."

"Yeah, listen up... let me go..."

Flaco leaned in closer and said, "...but get this, Manny yelled out one word and it was non-stop, even after they broke him down."

And in that moment, I no longer felt the need to leave and instead took a pause to ask, "What was that?"

Flaco looked around, cleared his throat, and then cupped his hand around his mouth and whispered, "Chankla."

TRANSLATIONS

- **Abuela:** Grandmother
- **Bata:** Spanish slang for a loose garment
- **Café con Leche:** Coffee with milk
- **Flaco:** Spanish word for skinny
- **Flamboyán:** Flamboyant tree usually found in Caribbean islands
- **High-waters:** English slang for pants with a long, noticeable gap between the hem and the top of the wearer's foot
- **Mofongo:** Puerto Rican dish containing plantains as its primary ingredient
- **Ya-Fe:** Fictional magic dust from the *Bodega Botanica* that grants wishes

LETTER TO THE READER

Dear Reader,

Thank you from the bottom of my *beating heart* for reading this story. The characters haunted me for years until I finally wrote the first phrase, "I met them". I wanted to find out who was the "them", and so the writing journey began. The fact that the story found its way into your hands has long been a dream of mine, and gives me chills to this day. I hope this story brought a little magic and acceptance into your life. If you'd like to stay connected and learn about my future tales, updates and exclusive content, I'd love to invite you to join the Bodega Botanica Newsletter. Also, **please leave a rating or review** on your favorite platform.

With gratitude,
Maria Rodriguez Bross

ACKNOWLEDGMENTS

Thank you to the following:

- Cover design by Julia Brooke Rothstein at juliabrooke.com
- Christine Vassos for the editing at vibrantediting.com
- Elba Caraballo for the Spanish translation
- AudioBook Contributors:
  - Fernando Figueroa Valladares for narration.
  - Brendon Pares at BB Media for audio editing.
  - Music was provided by CO.AG

My Family- I love you; you mean everything.

ABOUT THE AUTHOR

Maria Rodriguez Bross is an author, playwright, poet and blogger, whose work explores the unknown, the unexpected and the phenomenal. This is Maria's first short book, a novelette, which is the first in a six-part series. Maria's story-telling and personal blogging draws on the bilingual, multi-cultural world that shaped her. To learn more about Maria's writing, join the BBT Monthly Newsletter or visit her website, Bodega Botanica Tales.

goodreads.com/51945325

instagram.com/mariar.bross

amazon.com/stores/Maria-Rodriguez-Bross/author/B0DLVK6MS2

bookbub.com/profile/maria-rodriguez-bross

ALSO BY MARIA RODRIGUEZ BROSS

Bodega Botanica Tales: Carmen

Available for purchase on most book platforms